Some Other Books by Clyde Robert Bulla

THE BEAST OF LOR · BENITO · CHARLIE'S HOUSE

CONQUISTA! (WITH MICHAEL ROBERT SYSON)

DEXTER · THE DONKEY CART

DOWN THE MISSISSIPPI · EAGLE FEATHER

THE GHOST OF WINDY HILL · GHOST TOWN TREASURE

INDIAN HILL · JOHN BILLINGTON, FRIEND OF SQUANTO

JOHNNY HONG OF CHINATOWN · LAST LOOK

A LION TO GUARD US · MARCO MOONLIGHT

THE MOON SINGER · MY FRIEND THE MONSTER

OLD CHARLIE

OPEN THE DOOR AND SEE ALL THE PEOPLE

PIRATE'S PROMISE · POCAHONTAS AND THE STRANGERS

RIDING THE PONY EXPRESS · THE SECRET VALLEY

SHOESHINE GIRL · SONG OF ST. FRANCIS

SQUANTO, FRIEND OF THE PILGRIMS

STAR OF WILD HORSE CANYON

THE SUGAR PEAR TREE · SURPRISE FOR A COWBOY

THE SWORD IN THE TREE · VIKING ADVENTURE

WHITE BIRD · WHITE SAILS TO CHINA

THE WISH AT THE TOP

Clyde Robert Bulla

The Cardboard Crown

Illustrated by Michele Chessare

Thomas Y. Crowell   New York

Pe

The Cardboard Crown

Library of Congress Cataloging in Publication Data
Bulla, Clyde Robert.
  The cardboard crown.
  Summary: The life of an eleven-year-old farm boy
is changed when he meets an enchanting young stranger
from the city, the princess with the cardboard crown.
  [1. Friendship—Fiction] I. Chessare, Michele, ill.
II. Title
PZ7.B912Car 1984   [Fic]   83-45049
ISBN 0-690-04360-0
ISBN 0-690-04361-9 (lib. bdg.)

Designed by Al Cetta
1 2 3 4 5 6 7 8 9 10
First Edition

To Sandra Zevely

Contents

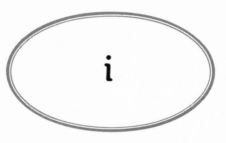

The Strange Evening

Supper was over. Adam lay on the floor, sorting his rock collection. His dog Rex curled up beside him. Adam's father lighted the lamp and sat down to read. The strange evening had begun.

Adam was restless. He didn't know why. Rex was restless, too. The old dog kept growling deep in his throat, until Adam's father looked up from his paper. "What are you doing to him?" he asked sharply.

"Nothing." Adam patted the dog's neck, and Rex was quiet.

Adam kept his collection in a shoebox. He had poured out all the rocks so he could see them better. He had thought he might throw some away—some that were not so good— but now he found he liked them all.

He was putting them back into the box when Rex growled again.

Father threw down his paper. "What's the *matter* with him?"

"I don't know. Maybe he hears another dog." Adam went to the door and looked out.

The summer night was clear. A bright moon, almost full, hung high over the woods. Its light turned the barn and sheds to silver.

A breeze blew in, and the lamplight flickered.

"Shut the door," said Father.

"I think Rex hears something," said Adam.

"There's nothing out there." Father stood up. He was a big man with heavy, black brows that gave him a frowning look.

Adam was big, too, for eleven. His shoulders were broad like his father's, but his hair was pale as cornsilk. No one had ever told him so, but he thought he must look more like his mother.

Father wound the clock. "Bedtime," he said.

Adam shut the door and knelt to pick up the rest of the rocks. Father looked down at them. "Are they going to make you a living?" he asked.

That was his way of saying, "What good are they?" Adam's face grew warm.

Suddenly Rex barked. As Adam and his father looked at each other, the front gate opened and closed.

Steps came up to the house. There was a knock.

[4]

Adam was near the door. He opened it. A girl stood outside. She was slim and small, and she wore a long, white dress. Her dark hair came to her shoulders. On her head was a golden crown.

She said something. It might have been "Good evening," or "May I come in?" Her voice was so low he couldn't be sure.

He stood aside, and she came in. Her dress made a whispering sound.

Adam could not take his eyes away from her. She was so beautiful. She was so young. There was such sadness in her face.

She sat down.

Rex had barked only once. He went toward her. She put out a hand. He sniffed it, then moved closer and let her stroke his head.

Adam's father spoke. "Who are you? What do you want?"

She only looked at him.

"What are you doing out here at night?"

His voice had grown louder. "What's that on your head?"

She reached up and touched the crown as if she had forgotten it was there. "I'm a princess," she said.

He looked startled. Then his mouth set. "You're from one of the neighbors', aren't you? Well, aren't you?"

"Oh, no," she answered.

"Have you—" Adam began, and stopped. He had almost asked if she had had her supper. It would have been a polite thing to say. But what was there in the house that was fit for a princess? Not cornbread. Not cold potatoes.

She said, "I'd like a drink of water."

He brought it to her in a flowered cup. She took a few sips.

"I'm very tired," she said. "Have you a place where I can rest?"

[6]

Father's mouth opened, but Adam spoke first.

"I'll show you," he said.

He lighted another lamp and led her into the spare room. It was their best room. He had always been rather proud of it, but now that she was seeing it, it began to look poor and plain. The wallpaper had faded. The floor was bare. Still, the bed was good. The sheets were clean, and the red and black cover had come from India.

She thanked him. He set the lamp on the dresser and left her.

Father said, "Why did you do that?"

"She looked so tired," said Adam.

"So you take her in when you don't know the first thing about her." Father sounded angry. "Coming here and calling herself a *princess*—"

"She *could* be, couldn't she?"

[7]

"No, she couldn't."

"Why not?"

"What would a princess be doing here by herself at this time of night?"

"She might be lost," said Adam.

"Then let her say so. Let her give an honest answer instead of all this playacting."

"How do you know it's playacting?"

"Look at those things she's wearing. They're for the stage, not for real life. Ten to one, that crown is cardboard. Don't you believe me?"

"I don't know."

"Why don't you ask her? Go ahead, ask her. If you won't, I will." Father started for the spare room.

Adam was at the door ahead of him. "Don't go in there."

"I *will* go in there."

"No," said Adam. He stood with his back to the door.

There was a stillness as they faced each other, then Father moved away. He stepped on a rock from Adam's collection and gave it a kick.

"Pick up those things," he said, "and get to bed!"

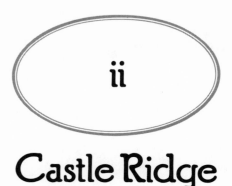

ii

Castle Ridge

Adam was first up in the morning. He had hardly slept all night.

There was a crack in the door of the spare room. He put his ear to it. He heard the soft sound of breathing.

He went into the kitchen and built a fire in the stove.

Father came out of the bedroom. "Is she still here?"

Adam nodded. "What about breakfast?"

"What about it?"

"She'll want something."

"You took her in. You can feed her." Father put the coffee on and began to stir up pancake batter.

"I wonder if she likes pancakes," said Adam.

"You can ask her, but you might not find out. She's not so good at giving straight answers."

They had breakfast—coffee for Father, milk for Adam, pancakes for them both.

After breakfast, Father went out. Adam washed the dishes. He went to the barn lot and fed the animals. He milked the cow.

Back in the house, he listened outside the spare room. This time he heard footsteps.

He hurried out to the kitchen and began to set the table. Before he had finished, the girl was in the doorway. Her head was up,

[11]

as if she were listening. Even without her crown, she looked like a princess.

She said, "Last night there was a man—"

"My father," he told her.

"Is he here?"

"Not now."

"I'm trying to remember," she said. "Did you tell me your name?"

"It's Adam."

"Adam." She smiled a little.

"What—" he began.

"Yes?"

"What about breakfast? We have things like milk and eggs—and pancakes."

She said, "If I could wash my face—"

He led her to the back door and showed her the washbasin on the shelf outside. He poured water for her and gave her a towel.

When she came in, she pushed back her hair and sat down at the table.

[12]

"I could make pancakes," he said.

"One," she said.

She ate the pancake he set before her. She drank the cup of milk. All the time she seemed to be listening.

"Are things safe here?" she asked. "In the woods, I mean."

"What things?"

"I left some things in the woods. Will they be all right, or should I get them?"

"I'll get them," said Adam.

"Oh, *would* you?"

"Tell me where they are."

"I'm not sure. I'll have to go with you."

They walked out into the barn lot.

A calf came around the corner of the barn. He stood in the sunlight and looked at them. Adam was proud. The calf was a yearling, the color of gold and cream. Even to a princess he would surely be beautiful.

The calf tossed his head.

"He won't hurt you," said Adam. "His name is Sultan, and he's mine. You don't see many like him. It's the color that makes him so different. People want to buy him, but he's not for sale. When he was born, he was little and puny, and we didn't think he would live, and my father gave him to me—"

Adam stopped. He had talked too much.

She was looking about the barn lot. She pointed to a wheelbarrow. "Can we take that?"

"What for?"

"To carry the things."

Adam pushed the wheelbarrow. He and the girl walked together into the woods.

"The things are under a tree by the road. I'll know the place when I see it." She asked, "Is this your land?"

"My father's."

"Where is the town?"

"What town?"

"There's a railroad station down below.

[15]

The sign on it says 'Castle Ridge.' Where is Castle Ridge?"

"*This* is Castle Ridge. It's just a long hill with farms on it. There isn't any town."

He had been looking along the ground. He said suddenly, "I found one!"

He showed her what he had found—a tiny evergreen tree.

"There aren't many evergreens here," he said, "and whenever I find one I dig it up and plant it—in a place I know about."

He marked the little tree with a stick.

The girl had gone on, and he caught up with her. They came to the road.

"That looks like the tree," she said. "Yes, it is."

It was an old oak with roots growing out of the ground. Among the roots were a brown leather bag and two boxes tied with string.

Adam loaded them onto the wheelbarrow.

"Are you tired?" he asked. "Do you want to rest?"

"No," she said.

But all at once she *seemed* tired. Her head was down. She let her dress drag in the wet grass as she walked along.

Back at the house, Adam opened the gate.

Father was on the porch. A woman was with him—a thin, gray scarecrow of a woman in a man's shirt and overalls. Adam knew her. She was Jen Painter, who lived alone on her farm up the road.

The girl saw her and gave a cry.

"So there you are," said the woman. "Out making trouble for people. But you don't care. No, *you* don't care!"

She swooped through the gate, caught the girl by the arm, and dragged her away.

The girl looked back at Adam. Her eyes were wild. He saw her mouth form the words, "Help me!"

[17]

A Secret Signal

It was a terrible sight—the girl twisting and pulling, the woman dragging her along.

Adam started after them, but Father held him.

"What's Jen doing?" cried Adam. "What right does she have—?"

"Slow down," said Father. "She has the right."

"*Why* does she?"

[18]

"Jen is her aunt."

The fight went out of Adam. Father let go of him.

Jen had dragged the girl down across the orchard and into the road. Already they were out of sight.

Father leaned against the gate. He looked pleased with himself. "I went to the Kesters', and I went to the Yorks'. They didn't know anything about the girl. And on the way home I met Jen. She was out looking for her niece from the city. She'd been looking since yesterday. I said, 'A little girl with a big imagination?' She said, 'That sounds like her,' and I said, 'I think we've got her.' "

"If she belonged at Jen's, why did she come to our house?" asked Adam.

"You said she might have got lost. Maybe she did."

"Then why didn't she ask us how to get to Jen's? And how did she get up here in the first place?" Adam was looking at the bag and boxes on the wheelbarrow. "She couldn't have carried these all by herself."

"You'll have to ask her," said Father. "And while you're asking, find out why she came here in those clothes and called herself a princess."

Adam was still looking at the wheelbarrow. "I'd better take these things to her."

"Not now," said Father. "This isn't the time."

It *wasn't* the time. Adam could see that.

He took the bag and boxes off the wheelbarrow. He carried them inside to the spare room where they would be safe and out of the way.

She had left her crown on the dresser. He picked it up. Father had said, "Ten to one, that crown is cardboard."

It *was* cardboard, painted gold.

[20]

Jen was back that afternoon. She came to the garden where Adam was hoeing potatoes.

They had been neighbors as long as he could remember, yet he hardly knew her. He hadn't *wanted* to know her. She lived by herself and kept to herself. *Old stone-face. Old scarecrow.* That was how he thought of her.

"Is your father home?" she asked.

"I'll go see." He hung the hoe on the fence. She went with him to the house.

Father was on the porch. "Come in, Jen."

"I can't stay. I just want you to know I'm sorry about last night, and I thank you for your trouble."

"No trouble," he said.

"Don't tell *me* it was no trouble. Having a stranger knock on your door after dark. Having to keep her overnight."

"I never would have guessed she was your

[22]

brother's girl," said Father. "I never knew he *had* a girl."

"There's a lot you never knew about my brother. He could charm you into thinking he was the finest fellow on earth, and underneath it all— Well." She drew in her breath. "I didn't come to talk about him. I came to fetch her things."

"Get them, Adam," said Father.

Adam brought the things from the spare room.

Father and Jen were still talking.

"It was just like my brother to do what he did yesterday," she was saying. "He wrote and asked if he could bring her. I said yes. Then he couldn't face me. He brought her up on The Ridge and left her to come the rest of the way by herself."

"And she got lost?" said Father.

"Maybe. I don't know. I put her to bed.

When she wakes up I'll try to get the whole story."

"Load these things and take them home for her, Adam," said Father.

Adam put the bag and boxes on the wheelbarrow. Jen went ahead, and he followed. He was surprised at how fast she could move. The deep lines across her forehead were what made her look so old. She was younger than he'd thought.

They went up the lane to her house. It was a tiny house, needing paint, hidden away behind trees and vines.

He unloaded the wheelbarrow on the front step. She went inside and came back with a dime that she tried to give him.

"No, thank you," he said.

"What's the matter? Isn't that enough?"

"I don't want any money." He was watching and listening.

"Well," said Jen, "don't let me keep you."

[24]

As he started away, he saw a curtain move in one of the windows. The girl was watching!

He put the wheelbarrow handles down and picked them up again. It was a secret signal. Jen wouldn't know what it meant, but the girl would know. *I'll be here*, he was saying. *I'll help you.*

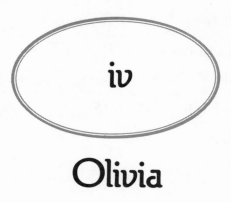

Olivia

The next day Father said they needed to make fence. Adam carried posts. Father dug holes. They were fencing the north pasture.

Toward the middle of the afternoon they stopped to rest and drink from the jug of water. Adam asked a question.

"Did you know Jen's brother?"

"I saw him around. I can't say I *knew* him.

He kept going to the city and coming back, and then he stayed."

"What did he do in the city?"

"He always said he was going to be an actor. . . . You know what that is, don't you?"

"I know. Did he get to be one?"

"I never saw his name in the papers."

"Jen didn't want him to go, did she?"

"She wanted him to stay and help her farm the land. That's what he should have done."

"Why?"

"Because he owed it to her, that's why. They were alone in the world. She brought him up—like a mother. She never got over it when he left her."

John York came by. He was their neighbor on the north.

"I saw you working," he said. "I thought I might give you a hand."

"Thanks, we can do this ourselves," Father told him.

[27]

But John York didn't go. "I guess you had some excitement at your house the other night."

And that was the real reason he'd come by, thought Adam—to find out about the girl.

"It was quite a surprise," said Father.

"Did you ever find out why she came to your house?" asked John York.

"I'll tell you what I think," said Father, and Adam knew there would be no more fence made that day.

He asked, "Shall I clean the shovel and take it in?"

"You can do that," said Father. "Take the jug, too."

Adam took the shovel and jug to the house. He washed his hands and face and changed his shirt. Then he headed up the road to Jen's.

Jen was in the yard, chopping firewood.

[28]

Sweat was running down her face. She gave him a long look from under the man's hat she was wearing.

"Could I see the girl?" he asked.

"What about?"

He had an answer ready. "She left something at our house."

"Livvie!" called Jen.

The girl came out. She wore a blue dress that looked faded and old. Her hair was pulled back and tied with a string. She wasn't a princess today.

"He wants to see you," said Jen.

The girl spoke to Adam. "Can we go over there, out of the sun?"

They sat on the grass in the shade of the lilac bush.

"Is that your name—Livvie?" he asked.

She made a face. "No. I hate it. I'm *Olivia*."

He said, "You left your crown at my house."

"My crown?"

"The one you had on."

"Oh. I don't want it."

Jen had gone back to her chopping.

"Look at her," said the girl. "Doesn't she look like a witch? And she *is* a witch. You wouldn't believe the things she's been saying. About my father. And she's got no right. He's a good man. He's a great actor, only he isn't famous. And he writes plays—wonderful plays—just for us. Just for him and me. Wherever we were, that was our theater. . . . You don't know what I'm saying, do you?"

"I think so."

"After Mother went away, there were just the two of us, and we made a wonderful life together. And all at once it was over. He said he was going on a journey—without me. He said I had to come here, where I'd be safe."

[30]

She pulled off a lilac leaf and tore it to pieces.

"He promised we'd have one last day together. He borrowed a car, and we drove all night and got to Castle Ridge in the morning. He didn't want to see Aunt Jen, and who could blame him? She came to the city once, and we were so *glad* when she went home." Olivia's voice was almost a whisper. "My father and I stopped in the woods, and we did all our plays out under the trees. We saved our favorite for the last. It was *The Lost Princess*. I was the princess. He was the king. He used his coat for a cape, and I had my costume in a box. In the end, the princess has to leave him. He tells her to go and not look back. That was how we said good-bye."

There were tears in her eyes. He started to say, "You don't have to talk about it," but she went on.

"Father had told me the way to Aunt Jen's, but I couldn't make myself go. I wandered around, and the sun went down. I still had my costume on, and I couldn't find where I'd left my things. Finally I did start toward Aunt Jen's. There were two lights. I didn't know which was hers—"

"And you came to ours," said Adam.

"Yes. When you let me stay, I thought maybe I could keep from going to Aunt Jen's. For a while, anyway. That's why I said what I did."

"About being a princess?"

She nodded. "I'd forgotten to take off my crown, and I didn't know what else to say. If I'd told who I was, your father would have taken me straight to Aunt Jen's, and I wasn't ready for her. I just wasn't *ready*. . . ."

"Livvie!" Jen was coming toward them. "You've sat long enough on that damp ground."

[33]

"I think she wants you to go." Olivia said quickly, "Adam, will you be my friend?"

Jen was coming nearer.

"Yes, I will," he said.

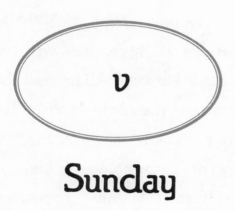

Sunday

One more day of making fence, then it was Sunday. Father had gone to the Yorks'. Adam was left alone.

Sunday was his day to go to the secret place. He really wanted to stop by to see Olivia, but it was probably too soon. Jen might send him home.

He started off to the secret place. In the

barn lot Sultan came to meet him. Adam put his face down against the calf's neck.

"You're my boy, aren't you?" he said.

Then Rex was there. Rex was trying to push his head between Adam and the calf.

Adam patted the old dog so he wouldn't feel left out. "You're my boy, too," he said.

They went on to the woods together. Rex ran after squirrels that didn't seem much afraid of him. Adam looked for evergreens. There weren't many on Castle Ridge. Father said a blight had killed them off. Lately they had started to grow back. Every now and then Adam came upon a small evergreen tree where the wind or a bird had planted it. Whenever he found one, he took it to the secret place.

Mother had told him, "Sometimes the world comes too close. Then you need a secret place where you can be quiet and alone."

Just before she died, she had told him that.

Adam had found his secret place in the

[36]

woods. It was near the high mound of rocks that looked like a castle and gave The Ridge its name.

Evergreens were hard to find. He gave up looking for them. He stopped in the shadow of the castle and looked for rocks instead.

He found only one worth keeping. It was small and smooth and red—such a deep red that it was almost black.

And as he picked it up, he saw an evergreen. He saw *two* evergreens! They were almost at his feet—two tiny trees.

With his pocket knife he carefully dug them up. He carried them, one in each hand, to the secret place.

It was a little, moon-shaped meadow in the middle of the woods. Around the edge he had planted his evergreens. Someday they would grow into a tall, dark ring.

He set out the trees. The little meadow was rocky, and there were springs among the rocks. He scooped up water in his hands and watered the new plants. All his trees were doing well. One was as high as his head. He counted them. There were seventeen.

Adam walked back. He felt the rock in his pocket. It might be a present for Olivia.

And when he and Rex got home, she was there!

She was sitting on the flatbed wagon in the barn lot.

"How long have you been here?" he asked.

"A long time. I was about to leave."

He sat beside her. "I'm glad you came over. Sunday gets to be a long day sometimes."

"Is it Sunday? That must be why Aunt Jen was sleeping late. Everything is so *quiet!*" she said. "How do you stand it? How do people *live* here?"

He was puzzled and a little hurt. "How do you mean?"

"There's nothing here. You're so far from everything."

"The train comes by."

"That's not what I mean. Don't you know about things like cars—or telephones—or electric lights?"

"We know about them," he said.

"You don't have them."

"We will someday, if we want them. It takes good roads for cars, and we don't have the roads for them yet. We had a telephone once, but we didn't use it much. We don't have electric lights because the electric line doesn't run this far."

She asked again, "How do you stand it?"

"We're used to things this way," he said. "Of course, I can see it's different for you."

"I'm glad you can see that."

"Maybe you won't have to stay long," he said. "Maybe your father will come back sooner than you think."

[40]

"Come back from where?"

"You said he was away on a trip."

"You didn't understand," she said. "You didn't understand at all. When my father told me he was going on a journey, he meant— he meant he was going to die."

Adam felt a chill. "How do you know he meant that?"

"It's what he *had* to mean! Why else would he have brought me here and left me? Oh, I don't know why I go on talking about it." She slid down off the wagon. "Good-bye."

"Wait."

"I have to go. Aunt Jen doesn't know where I am. She'll be sending the police after me. But I forgot. You don't have any police, do you?"

He watched her go. Why was she so *different* today?

He remembered the rock in his pocket. He

was glad he hadn't given it to her. What would a rock from him mean to someone like Olivia? Probably something to throw away as soon as she was out of sight.

Trouble

Adam and his father had gone to bed. Adam was in his cot by the window. Father was in the big bed across the room.

Father said, "That girl was here this morning, wasn't she?"

"Yes," answered Adam.

"I thought so. John York and I saw her coming this way. What did she want?"

"Just to talk."

"Couldn't she talk to her aunt?"

"I don't suppose she has much to say to Jen."

"That girl is trouble. I can't see her as anything else." Father turned over in bed. Soon he was snoring.

Adam lay awake. He heard Rex on the porch. The old dog was half-growling, half-whining. They were the sounds he made when something was wrong. In a moment he would bark and wake Father.

Adam got into his clothes and went outside. He put his hand on the dog's throat. "Don't bark," he whispered.

Now he could hear what Rex must have heard. Someone was walking toward the house. The gate clicked open and shut.

"Who is it?" he asked.

"Adam?" It was Olivia's voice. "I can't see you. It's so dark."

He went inside. He bumped into a chair

before he found the matches. He lighted a lamp and set it on the table by the window.

He and Olivia sat on the porch in the lamp-light.

"I want to stay here tonight," she said.

"What's the matter?"

"It's Aunt Jen. She keeps saying I have to know the truth."

"The truth?"

"About my father. So I won't grow up like him. Adam, I *know* about my father. Maybe he's not perfect, but who is? I don't need her to keep telling me—"

"Adam, where are you?" Father was calling from inside the house. "Did you light the lamp?" He came to the doorway. "Who's out there?"

"Olivia," said Adam.

"Who?"

"The girl from Jen's."

"What does she want?"

Olivia stood up. "I came to ask a favor. I want to stay here tonight."

"Well, you can't," he said.

"Why can't she?" asked Adam.

"Because we don't want trouble." Father spoke to Olivia. "I don't know what's between you and your aunt, and I don't want to know. I'm not taking sides. If I took you in, I would be."

"I wouldn't come in," she said. "I'd sleep out here."

"That would be the same thing."

She turned slowly. She stepped down off the porch.

Father hesitated. "Better go with her, Adam. Take the lantern. See that she gets home all right."

They cut across the orchard and walked up the road. Adam carried the lantern. Olivia's face was pale in the light.

"So I've made trouble again," she said.

"No."

"Yes, I have. I always do. I was awful to you today. Sometimes I feel so *twisted*. And when I went back, I had to face Aunt Jen. Where had I been? Why hadn't I told her where I was going? Oh, it's been a day!"

"Jen isn't used to having anybody around. Maybe when she's used to you, things will get better."

"Things will not get better. Tonight I shut myself up in my room to get away from her, and I heard one of those birds—what is it?— a whippoorwill. It was the saddest sound I ever heard, and it wouldn't stop. I nearly went out of my mind, and I climbed out the window and came to your house— Adam, help me. Help me get away."

"Didn't your father mean for you to stay?"

"He wouldn't want me to stay if he knew how things are."

"Where would you go?"

[47]

"To Lady Alice's. She's a friend of my father's. That's what we call her—Lady Alice. If I can get to the city, she'll take me in. I know she will. And if my father is in a hospital, she'll know how to find him. There's a train going north. I hear it every morning before I'm up. I could take that train. But I haven't any money. Do you have any money?"

"No," he answered.

"Can you get some?"

"I don't know where."

They had come to the lane that led to Jen's house.

"You'd better not come any farther," she said. "I left the window open. I'll try to get in so she won't hear me."

Her voice had changed. It sounded hopeless and tired. Before he could think of anything more to say, she was gone.

He hadn't helped. For all his promises, there was nothing he could do.

On his way home, the lantern went out. He shook it. It was out of oil.

He walked along in the dark. A whip-poorwill was crying—more than likely the same one Olivia had heard. She must be hearing it, too. And while he listened, the idea came to him. He wondered why he hadn't thought of it before. Probably because he hadn't *wanted* to think of it. He didn't want to think of it now.

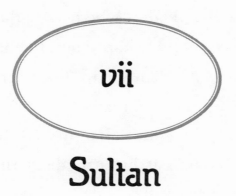

Sultan

All the next day he turned it over in his mind. By evening he could still see no other way.

Father asked at supper, "Not hungry?"

"Not very," said Adam.

He finished his chores. The long evening was left.

He sat on the flatbed wagon in the barn lot. He knew Sultan would be coming up to him. He closed his eyes and waited, and Sultan was there, pushing at him with his nose.

Adam had the rope ready. He slipped it over the calf's head.

He didn't know whether Father was watching or not. He hoped not, but he didn't try to hide. He led Sultan down across the pasture and into the road.

Adam had taught Sultan to lead, but part of the way he put his arm about the calf's neck and they walked side by side.

They came to Sam Kester's. Sam was sitting in a chair in the yard. He was old and he chewed tobacco and he smiled all the time. Some said he wasn't quite right in the head, but that wasn't true. Sam was sharp.

He came out to the road.

Adam said, "I brought my calf."

Sam nodded. "I see you did."

"Remember what I told you?"

"What was that?"

[52]

"I told you if I ever wanted to sell Sultan, I'd give you first chance."

"Well, now—" A greedy look came into the old man's eyes. "Well, now, I don't know. Did you talk to your father?"

"I didn't need to," said Adam. "Sultan is mine."

"What do you want for him?"

"What will you give me?"

"I'll give you what's right." Sam reached into his pocket and took out a little bag. "I've got some money here—" He counted bills into Adam's hand. "There. How does that look to you?"

"Is there enough to ride the train to the city?"

"Are you fixing to ride the train?"

"No," said Adam, "but is it enough?"

"More than enough, I should say."

"It's all right, then." Adam handed the

[53]

rope over to Sam and walked away. He knew Sultan was pulling at the rope, wanting to go with him, and he didn't want to see. He walked faster, without looking back.

He went straight to Jen's.

Jen and Olivia were at the woodpile. Jen had cut some wood and was showing Olivia how to carry it.

"Lay the sticks on your arm—like this." Jen saw Adam. "Here's somebody who can maybe show you better than I can."

He knelt by the woodpile. Olivia watched him lay sticks on his arm until he had a load.

"I might as well take this in," he said.

She opened the back door for him. He went past her into the kitchen and dumped the wood into the woodbox. She was still in the doorway. He had hoped for this—a moment alone with her.

He held out the money. She gazed at it, her mouth open.

"Take it!"

She took the bills and hid them in her hand.

He went outside. She came running after him.

"Will you—will you show me again?" she asked.

He picked up another load of wood. "Don't try to take too much," he said. He carried it inside. She followed him.

"The money," she said. "Are you sure?"

"I'm sure."

"Where did you get it?"

"It doesn't matter."

"Yes, it does. I'm afraid—"

"I sold my calf," he said.

"Oh . . . Adam, when I go, I'll need some help. Will you help me get to the station?"

"When?"

"I don't know. Maybe tomorrow. Yes, to-morrow!"

"All right," he said.

"Be down by the road. I'll get the morning train."

Jen came in.

"We thank you for carrying in the wood," she said. "Sit yourself down and I'll bring you some buttermilk and cookies."

"Thanks, I'll get on home," he said. He didn't look at her as he hurried out the door.

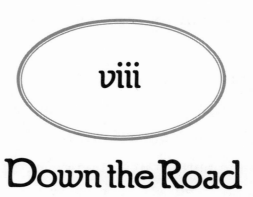

Down the Road

They met by the lane that led to Jen's house. Olivia had been running, and she was out of breath.

"Just a minute," she said.

He heard a rooster crow. He saw the clouds turning pink across the east.

She was dragging something out of the weeds by the roadside. "I hid this here last night."

It was the leather bag. He picked it up.

"Are we late?" she asked. "I couldn't get away. Aunt Jen was up, wandering around. I thought she'd *never* go back to bed. I think she suspects something. Adam, let's run!"

They ran. The bag was heavy. He was glad the road was all downhill.

They found the railroad track and followed it. They came to the station and went inside.

A sleepy-eyed man sold Olivia her ticket. He stared at them until Adam felt strange.

"Let's go out," he said.

He and Olivia waited on the platform. She looked different this morning. Every day she seemed different. How many Olivias were there? Which one was real? He'd never know, because he'd never see her again.

The train whistled at the far end of The Ridge. They could see it winding over the flatlands. It came in with a rush and a roar.

Olivia got on. He handed the bag up to her.

"Good-bye," he said.

She was inside. He saw her go past a window, and the train was moving. It was gone. He didn't know whether she had said good-bye or not.

When Adam got home, Father was in the barn lot feeding the pigs. Feeding the pigs was one of Adam's chores.

"I'll do it," he said. He picked up the corn basket.

"Where have you been?" asked Father.

"At the station," answered Adam.

"What was there that got you up before daylight?"

"Olivia went away on the train."

"Was she running away?"

"She wasn't used to things here," said Adam.

[61]

"I asked you—was she running away?"

"Yes."

"And you helped her?"

"I carried her bag."

"You helped her, behind Jen's back. Behind my back, too. You took sides against your neighbor. Come on. We're going to Jen's."

"Why?" asked Adam.

"You're going to tell her everything that happened."

But there was no need to go to Jen's. She was there, coming across the barn lot.

"Livvie's gone!" she cried.

Just in that moment Adam felt sorry for her. He couldn't help it. She looked so *lost*.

Father said, "Adam here can tell you all about it."

"She went on the train," Adam said.

Jen looked into his face. "Are you sure?"

"I was with her. She's on her way home."

"Home? She hasn't *got* a home, except here. They'll put her off the train. That child didn't have any money."

"She had some."

"How do you know?"

"I got it for her."

"Better come in the house, Jen," said Father. "We'll talk about this." He took hold of her arm.

She pulled away. She went off across the barn lot.

Adam had put down the corn basket. Now he picked it up again.

"Just a minute," said Father. "*Did* you get money for that girl?"

"Yes."

"Where?"

"I sold Sultan."

"You *what*?"

"I sold my calf."

"Who bought him?"

"Sam Kester."

"So. You and Sam made a little deal behind my back."

"Sultan was mine," said Adam. "You said so."

"And you gave the money to that girl so she could run away?"

"Yes."

Father said very slowly, "Sometimes it seems to me that you're no son of mine."

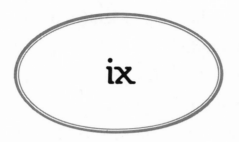

ix

Night and Morning

Adam finished the chores. By that time Father was nowhere in sight. Rex was gone, too. He was probably visiting the neighbors' dogs, as he sometimes did.

Adam took his hoe and went to the cornfield. The morning passed, and most of the afternoon, and he worked alone.

When suppertime came, he went to the house. There were crumbs on the kitchen table. Father had already eaten and was gone again. Now Adam knew. He was being shut out.

He did the milking and fed the animals, and he thought about Sultan. At feeding time the calf had always been there, pushing at the gate with his nose.

Did Sultan miss him, too? How long would a calf remember?

He had his supper—a bowl of bread and milk. It was still daylight. He walked through the woods to the secret place.

The little meadow was quiet and cool. He lay on the grass and looked at the sky. Night came, and still he lay there, not wanting to go home. It was almost as if he *had* no home.

". . . you're no son of mine," Father had said. ". . . no son of mine."

He wondered where Olivia was. Would she write him a letter? He didn't suppose she would. No one had ever written him a letter.

Two owls were crying—one near, one far. He listened to them, and after a long time he fell asleep.

It was daylight when he woke. Father was standing over him. It was like a dream, but it was real.

"Are you all right?" asked Father.

Adam sat up. "How did you—"

"How did I what?"

"I didn't know you knew about this place."

Father gave a short laugh. "Oh, I knew about it. Hadn't you better come home?"

They went home.

"Better go to bed for a while," Father told him.

"I slept last night," said Adam.

"Sleeping on the ground doesn't do you as much good," said Father.

So Adam went to bed, and he slept.

[67]

The next day they were back in the corn-field. They were both quiet, and they hoed without looking at each other.

Toward noon Jen came out to the field. She had been crying. Adam had never thought Jen could cry.

She said, "I keep bothering you—"

"No bother," said Father. "What can I do for you?"

She turned to Adam. "When you get time, I wish you'd fetch Livvie's bag. She left it at the station."

"She didn't leave it," said Adam. "She took it with her."

"Livvie came back."

Adam stood still.

"She came in on the train last night and left her things at the station. That's all I know. She won't talk. She won't eat—"

"I'll fetch the bag," said Adam.

[68]

"And maybe," Jen said, "maybe you could talk to her."

Adam took the bag to Jen's. She let him in.

"I thank you for your help."

"Where is she?" asked Adam.

"In there." Jen nodded toward a closed door. She called, "Livvie! Somebody's here to see you."

There was no answer.

"When she came in last night she looked as if something terrible had happened." Jen called again, "Livvie!"

Still there was no answer.

"Would you try, Adam? Get her to come out if you can."

He put his face to the door. "Olivia, it's Adam."

The door opened suddenly. Olivia looked out. Her face had gone sharp and strange.

[70]

"If you want your money," she said, "I haven't got it."

"I *don't*—" he began.

"Just go away and leave me alone," she said, and she shut the door.

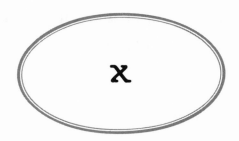

X

The Evergreen

Adam found his hoe where he had left it. Father had moved on to the far end of the field. When he saw Adam, he came back.

"She didn't stay long, did she?"

"No," said Adam.

"Looks as though you had all your trouble for nothing. What did she come back for?"

"I don't know."

"Didn't you see her?"

"Yes."

"What did she say?"

"Leave me alone!" said Adam, and he threw down his hoe and walked out of the field.

The rest of the week was long. Adam and his father worked together, they were in the house together, yet they hardly spoke.

On Sunday Adam went to the secret place. Rex went with him. While the old dog nosed among the bushes, Adam sat on a rock and tried to think.

He had disappointed his father. He could see that and understand it. But why had Olivia turned against him? What had he done except try to help?

Maybe he shouldn't have tried. Maybe he wouldn't ever try again. Wouldn't it be better if he went along with his head down and didn't care about anything or anybody?

Rex gave one short bark.

[73]

Adam looked up. There at the edge of the meadow was Olivia.

He didn't move. She came toward him. She had something in her hand—a tiny evergreen in a nest of earth.

She was beautiful again. There was still that sadness in her eyes, but she was smiling.

He got up as she held out the evergreen.

He took it. "Where did you get this?"

"In Aunt Jen's pasture. I was going to bring it yesterday, but she said you might be coming over."

"How did you know where I was?"

"Your father told me. He didn't want to, but he finally did. He said you *might* be in this little place on the other side of Castle Rock. Now I see. This is where you plant the evergreens."

"It's my secret place," he said, "only it isn't very secret anymore."

"I thought you'd come over yesterday," she said.

"After you told me to go away and leave you alone?"

"That was how I felt then. Didn't you ever want to be alone?"

He remembered what he'd said to his father. "Yes, I guess I have. But you acted as if I wanted the money."

"I knew better than that. I was feeling so awful, I must have wanted you to feel awful, too."

"I hope you found your father," he said. "I hope he was all right."

"He wasn't dying, if that's what you mean. I found him at Lady Alice's, and he certainly wasn't dying. I was wrong about that. Do you want to know what happened?"

He shook his head.

"I want to tell you. It's funny. I don't tell

[75]

Aunt Jen anything, and I tell you everything. My father wanted Lady Alice to marry him. She wouldn't, as long as I was there. He wanted me, but he wanted her more. But he couldn't tell me that. He just left me at Aunt Jen's. When I went to Lady Alice's, he wouldn't even talk to me. She was the one who had to tell me. When she sent me back, she said, 'You're young. You'll get over this.' She was probably right. Only you don't know what it's like when your own father—" She stopped.

"Maybe I do know," said Adam. "My father shuts me out. I'm shut out now."

"But he'd never send you away."

"He might if he could."

"No. Maybe you worry him. Maybe he doesn't know what to do with you, but he wants you."

"You don't know that."

"Yes, I do. Listen. I talked to him this

morning. I asked him if he'd buy back your calf—"

"You *what*?"

"I said if he could buy it back I'd pay him, a little at a time. He said even if he could, you wouldn't take it. He said, 'When that boy makes a deal, he stands by it.' The way he said it—he was proud of you."

Adam heard the words. He turned them over in his mind. He couldn't quite believe them yet. But they *might* be true.

He told her, "Maybe you don't know this, but somebody wants you, too. Jen wants you."

Olivia said slowly, "You know, I think she does. I can't imagine why. I'm not easy to live with. I have a temper. I pretend a lot. At first I hated her for the things she said about my father, even when I knew some of them were true, but maybe she was trying to make me understand—Adam, I *will* pay you back."

"I don't want to be paid back."

"I asked Aunt Jen how I could get some money. She said I could raise chickens and sell eggs. Did you ever hear of anything so crazy?" She began to laugh. She was crying a little, too. "I'll go out of my mind here. What is there to *do*?"

"For one thing," he said, "there'll be school."

"There will?"

"We go to school here on The Ridge."

"I never thought about school," she said.

"The schoolhouse isn't far. I'll show it to you. We can look in the windows. It has just one room. Last year there were seven girls and six boys."

"It sounds awful."

"Miss Larson is a pretty good teacher." He remembered something. "We give plays at school."

"You do?" She looked interested. "What kind?"

"Out of books. Or we make up our own."

She walked away from him, around the evergreen ring. "You know what this is like? It's like a theater. Where the rocks are, this is the stage."

She stood on a rock. She turned her face toward the sky and lifted her arms.

"Do you still have my crown?" she asked.

"Yes."

"Save it for me, Adam," she said.

About the Author

Clyde Robert Bulla is one of America's best-known writers for young people. The broad scope of his interests has led him to write more than fifty distinguished books on a variety of subjects, including travel, history, science, and music. He has received a number of awards for his contributions to the field of children's books, including, for *Shoeshine Girl*, awards in three states—Oklahoma, Arkansas, and South Carolina—the winners of which were voted upon by school children.

Clyde Bulla's early years were spent on a farm near King City, Missouri. He now lives and works in the bustling city of Los Angeles. When he is not busy writing a book, he loves to travel.